Sherlock Holmes and The Baker Street Thefts

Mabel Swift

Sherlock Holmes and The Baker Street Thefts

(A Sherlock Holmes Mystery - Book 4)

By

Mabel Swift

Copyright 2024 by Mabel Swift

www.mabelswift.com

All rights reserved. No part of this publication may be reproduced in any form, electronically or mechanically without permission from the author.

This is a work of fiction and any resemblance to any person living or dead is purely coincidental.

Contents

Chapter 1	1
Chapter 2	6
Chapter 3	12
Chapter 4	17
Chapter 5	23
Chapter 6	32
Chapter 7	35
Chapter 8	39
Chapter 9	45
Chapter 10	49
Chapter 11	52
Chapter 12	57
Chapter 13	60
A note from the author	64

Sherlock Holmes and the Lamplighter's Mystery - a preview 66

Chapter 1

It was early afternoon, and inside 221B Baker Street, Sherlock Holmes was reading a mystery novel and occasionally shaking his head at the unlikely plot twists within the story. His companion, Dr John Watson, sat across from him, a newspaper on his lap. Dr Watson's eyes were closed and a light series of snores came from him.

The tranquil scene was suddenly shattered by the sound of hurried footsteps on the stairs, followed by a frantic knock at the door.

"Come in, Mrs Hudson," Holmes called out, recognising her knock.

Dr Watson snorted, opened his eyes and blinked. "What? What was that? What's going on?"

The door burst open, revealing their landlady, Mrs Hudson, her face flushed with agitation. "Mr Holmes, Dr Watson! Thank goodness you're both here."

Watson turned to look at their landlady. "Whatever is the matter, Mrs Hudson?"

"There are thefts taking place! Right here on Baker Street!" she exclaimed. "I've just heard about them from my neighbour, and I fear our home may be targeted next. Whatever shall we do?"

Holmes closed the book he was reading and placed it on the table next to him. "Thefts? Pray tell us more, Mrs Hudson. Please, sit down."

Mrs Hudson took a seat across from the two men. "My neighbour, Vera Wilkins, was telling me all about it. Apparently, there have been several incidents of valuable items going missing from various households on our very street."

"What sort of items?" Watson inquired.

"It seems to be jewellery," Mrs Hudson replied. "This morning, she saw the Thompsons on their doorstep discussing a missing brooch. They live further up the road, and on the opposite side. Anyway, Vera was walking past them on her way to the shops. Mrs Thompson was upset about something and her voice was quite loud. Well, Vera couldn't help but hear what they were saying, could she?"

Holmes smiled. "I suppose not. And what did Mr and Mrs Thompson have to say about this missing brooch?"

"Mr Thompson seemed to think it might have simply been misplaced," Mrs Hudson explained, "but Mrs Thompson was adamant it was on her dressing table because she always kept it there, but when she looked for it that morning, intending to wear it, it was gone. Mrs Thompson had searched her bedroom, but it was nowhere to be found."

Watson reached for his pocketbook and made a note about the incident.

"And then there's Mrs Henderson," Mrs Hudson continued, "who noticed a pearl necklace missing from her jewellery box a few days before."

"And how do you know about that?" Holmes asked.

Mrs Hudson replied, "Mrs Henderson told me. I was walking through the park yesterday as it was such a lovely day, and I saw Mrs Henderson sitting on a bench. She didn't look like her normal happy self at all. So, I asked if something was wrong. She told me about the missing necklace. She said she always keeps it in the jewellery box when she's not wearing it. But it's no longer there. She thinks she might have put it somewhere else for some reason, but now can't remember where she put it. She thinks she's losing her memory. Poor woman. I tried to be positive and said, these things turn up in unexpected places sometimes."

"That's true," Watson said. "I hope she finds that necklace soon."

Mrs Hudson's eyes narrowed. "The thing is, Dr Watson, I think it's been stolen, and I think Mrs Thompson's brooch has been stolen, too." She paused. "Someone else has noticed a missing piece of jewellery on this street, Mrs Baxter. She's lost some diamond earrings. And this happened last week, according to Vera, who is friends with Mrs Baxter's sister. Three missing items, all from people who live on this street. And they all occurred within the last few weeks. These are not coincidences. Not at all. And I know your feelings on coincidences, Mr Holmes."

"Indeed," Holmes replied. "I don't believe in them. Mrs Hudson. I agree these incidents are not coincidences, but evidence of something else taking place. Those missing items are small and easily transportable. This suggests a thief who is adept at moving swiftly and undetected."

"Precisely my thoughts, Mr Holmes," Mrs Hudson agreed. "I don't have many valuables, but the ones I have are very precious to me. And I know you two have items of value, too. With the thefts occurring so close to home, I'm worried that we may be the next targets."

"We shall take every precaution to ensure that does not happen," Holmes assured her. "Watson and I will look into this matter, and we will do so immediately."

Mrs Hudson sighed with relief. "I'm so glad to hear that, Mr Holmes, so very glad."

Holmes turned to Watson, a determined glint in his eye. "Watson, we shall pay a visit to the Thompsons and inquire about this missing brooch. It seems the most recent incident, and therefore, the one with the freshest trail to follow. Mrs Hudson, could you give me the house numbers of where Mrs Thompson and the other ladies live, please?"

"Of course." Mrs Hudson gave Holmes the required information.

As the two men prepared to depart, Mrs Hudson rose from her seat, a grateful smile on her face. "Thank you, gentlemen. I feel much better knowing you're on the case."

Holmes offered her a reassuring nod. "Have no fear, Mrs Hudson. We shall uncover the truth behind these thefts and ensure the perpetrator is brought to justice."

With that, the famous detective and his trusted companion set off, ready to make their investigations.

Chapter 2

Minutes later, Sherlock Holmes and Dr Watson approached the ornate front door of the building where Mr and Mrs Thompson lived.

Holmes rapped on the door, and a few seconds passed before it swung open, revealing a young woman in a crisp maid's uniform.

"Good afternoon, sirs," she greeted, her tone polite but guarded. "How may I be of assistance?"

Holmes offered a warm smile. "Good day, miss. I am Sherlock Holmes, and this is my colleague, Dr John Watson. We're here to speak with Mrs Thompson regarding a rather delicate matter."

The maid's expression softened slightly, and she nodded. "Of course, Mr Holmes. Do come in." She ushered them inside, leading them through the foyer and into an elegantly appointed sitting room. "If you'll excuse me for a moment, I'll inform Mrs Thompson of your arrival."

As the maid departed, Watson leaned in closer to Holmes. "What are your initial observations, Holmes?"

Holmes scanned the room, taking in every detail. "The household appears well-kept, with no obvious signs of disarray or disturbance. I didn't see any signs of a forced entry on the main door or the front-facing windows. However, we mustn't draw any premature conclusions until we've spoken with Mrs Thompson herself."

Moments later, the maid returned, followed by a woman in her late fifties. Mrs Thompson was impeccably dressed, her greying hair styled in an elegant coiffure, and her demeanour exuded a sense of refinement and poise.

"Mr Holmes, Dr Watson," she greeted, her voice tinged with a hint of concern. "I understand you wished to speak with me about a delicate matter."

Holmes inclined his head respectfully. "We do, Mrs Thompson. We've been made aware of a recent incident involving a missing brooch belonging to yourself, and we were hoping you could provide us with more details."

Mrs Thompson's expression grew grave, and she motioned for them to take a seat. "Ah, yes, the brooch. A most distressing situation, I must say. It was a family heirloom, passed down through generations, and of immense sentimental value. I had placed it on my dressing table, as I always do after wearing it. I wished to wear it this morning, but when I looked for the brooch, it was gone."

Watson smiled gently, "Forgive me for asking, but are you certain it wasn't simply misplaced? These things do happen."

Mrs Thompson shook her head firmly. "I am meticulous in my habits, and I can assure you that the brooch was precisely where I always left it. I wear it most days and like to have it to hand when needed."

Holmes nodded. "And have you noticed any other items missing from your home, or any signs of a potential break-in?"

"Not that I'm aware of, Mr Holmes," Mrs Thompson replied. "The house appears undisturbed, and nothing else seems to be missing. It's as if the brooch simply vanished into thin air."

Holmes said, "Mrs Thompson, we've been informed that there have been other incidents of missing valuables on this very street. Are you aware of this?"

Mrs Thompson frowned. "No, I am not aware of that. Have these items vanished as mysteriously as mine?"

"It appears so," Holmes confirmed.

"May I ask, who has reported these incidents?" Mrs Thompson said.

"They haven't been reported as such," Holmes replied. "But the information has come to us via contacts. It seems Mrs Henderson has lost a pearl necklace, and Mrs Baxter has lost a pair of diamond earrings."

Mrs Thompson gasped. "No! But I am friends with those ladies. We meet almost every day for lunch. They never told me about their missing jewellery."

"Perhaps they thought the items had been misplaced and they would find them soon," Holmes offered.

Mrs Thompson nodded slowly. "Ah, yes, that could be the case. My husband thinks I've misplaced my brooch. We had quite the animated discussion on the doorstep this morning about it. I'm surprised the neighbours didn't hear us." Comprehension dawned on her face and she broke into a smile. "One of the neighbours did hear us, though, didn't she? I noticed Mrs Wilkins going by, and how her steps slowed when she passed our home. And Mrs Wilkins is a good friend of your lovely landlady. Now, I understand how you know about my brooch."

Holmes bowed his head a little. "Yes, people are prone to discuss their neighbour's lives. This information was passed to us with honest intentions, and not as malicious gossip, I assure you."

Mrs Thompson waved a hand dismissively. "I can see that, Mr Holmes. And I'm glad the information was passed to you. Can I assume you will look into this matter on my behalf?"

"Of course," Holmes replied. "We will investigate this mystery thoroughly, and we will find the person behind it. You have my word. Furthermore, we will do our utmost to reunite you with your brooch.

Mrs Thompson clasped her hands together, her eyes shining with relief. "Oh, Mr Holmes, I cannot begin to express my gratitude. This brooch means the world to me, and the thought of losing it forever is simply unbearable."

Holmes rose from his seat, offering Mrs Thompson a reassuring smile. "We shall leave no stone unturned in our investigation. If any further information comes to your mind about this mystery, no matter how insignificant it may seem, I implore you to share it with us."

Mrs Thompson nodded, her expression resolute. "Of course, Mr Holmes. Anything to aid in the recovery of my beloved brooch."

"One more thing before we go. May we speak with your maid, the one who answered the door? She may have noticed someone unusual hanging around recently. Perhaps someone who was showing an interest in your home, and those of your neighbours."

Mrs Thompson said, "Matilda? Oh, of course. Yes, please do speak to her. She'll be in the kitchen at this time of the day."

"Thank you, we will seek her out. How long has Matilda worked for you?" Holmes asked.

Mrs Thompson smiled. "Ten years. She's like part of the family. I don't know what I'd do without her."

Chapter 3

Sherlock Holmes and Dr Watson left the sitting room and headed to the kitchen, where Matilda was placing some freshly cooked scones on a cooling rack.

Holmes cleared his throat. "Please excuse our intrusion, but may we speak to you, Matilda? We won't take up much of your time."

For a second, Matilda looked startled to see them, but then she smiled and said, "Of course. Won't you sit down?" She gestured towards the small table in the corner. "Can I get you anything to eat or drink?"

"Not for me." Holmes said as he sat down.

"Me neither, but thank you," Dr Watson said, taking a seat next to Holmes. He reached into his pocket and retrieved his notebook and pen.

Matilda moved away from the cooling rack and sat opposite them, expectation in her eyes.

Holmes said, "We have been asked to look into the disappearance of Mrs Thompson's brooch. Are you aware it has gone missing?"

Matilda nodded. "Yes, Mrs Thompson is ever so upset about it. I helped her look for it. We've searched this house from top to bottom, we have." She paused and studied Holmes more closely. "But you don't think it's been lost, do you, Mr Holmes? I know you're a detective. You wouldn't look into a brooch that's been lost. Do you think it's been stolen?"

Holmes answered, "The question is, do you think it's been stolen?"

She gave them a slow nod. "I do, but I'm not sure how. I'm friends with some of the other maids on this street, and they've told me that items belonging to their employees have also gone missing. It's too much of a coincidence to be, well, an actual coincidence, isn't it? There's something funny going on."

"Who do your friends work for?" Dr Watson asked.

"Betsy works for Mrs Henderson, and Enid works for Mrs Baxter." She cast a glance towards the kitchen door. "Mrs Thompson is friends with those other ladies, and they meet up nearly every day."

Holmes said, "Yes, Mrs Thompson was kind enough to share that information with us. Tell me, is the house empty during the day?"

"It is. Mrs Thompson usually goes out at eleven in the morning. She returns about two or three in the afternoon. She hasn't been out today because she's so upset about her brooch. I really don't like to see her like that." Matilda fell silent and stared at the table.

"And what about you, Matilda?" Holmes asked. "Do you leave the house during the day?"

Matilda looked up. "Yes, I do. I have chores that take me out of the house, like shopping, collecting cleaning, delivering messages on behalf of Mr and Mrs Thompson, that sort of thing. I make sure Mrs Thompson has everything she needs before she leaves at eleven, and after that I'll leave and get on with my chores. I make sure I'm back about one o'clock so that I can make a start on afternoon refreshments for when Mrs Thompson returns."

Dr Watson made some notes in his book. He looked up and said, "So, the house is normally empty between eleven and one? Is that right?"

"It is." Matilda's eyes widened. "Oh! Is that when you think the brooch was stolen?"

"It is a window of opportunity," Holmes replied.

Matilda frowned. "But how would they get in? I always make sure everything is locked up properly. And I haven't seen any damaged locks or broken windows."

"How someone gained entry is something we'll find out in due course," Holmes said. "Have you noticed anything out of the ordinary around the house in recent days? Any strange occurrences or visitors that might be connected to the theft?"

"Not that I can recall," Matilda replied, shaking her head. "The comings and goings have been much the same as always."

Holmes pressed on, "Who are the regular visitors to this household?"

Matilda paused, gathering her thoughts. "Well, there's Mrs Thompson's circle of friends, of course. Ladies like Mrs Henderson and Mrs Baxter, whom she mentioned to you earlier. They often stop by for tea or to discuss the latest society gossip. But mostly, they prefer to meet at cafés or restaurants."

Watson interjected, "And do any of these ladies have a particular interest in jewellery or valuable items?"

"Not that I'm aware of," Matilda said with a frown. "They're all well-to-do ladies, of course, but I've never known any of them to be overly interested in such things."

Holmes nodded, his expression thoughtful. "And what about deliveries or tradespeople? Are there any regular visitors of that nature?"

"Yes, Mr Holmes," Matilda replied. "We have the usual deliveries of food and household goods. And there's the chimney sweep, who comes by every few months to clean the flues."

Watson asked, "And have there been any new faces around the household recently? Any visitors or tradespeople out of the ordinary?"

Matilda nodded and opened her mouth to respond, but before she could utter a word, a sharp knock echoed from the back door. Her eyes widened, and a flicker of fear crossed her features as she glanced towards the frosted glass pane where a man's silhouette was visible.

Chapter 4

With a steadying breath, Matilda stood up and crossed the kitchen. She opened the door, revealing a person clad in the attire of a milkman.

"Jimmy," Matilda greeted stiffly, her tone devoid of warmth.

The man grinned, his glance roving over her in a manner that made her shift uncomfortably. "Well now, don't you look pretty today, Matilda." He stepped briskly into the kitchen without an invitation. "Lovely day, ain't it? Got any plans for the rest of the afternoon?"

Matilda retreated a few paces. "Just my usual duties, Jimmy. Nothing out of the ordinary."

"Is that so?" Jimmy's gaze drifted towards Holmes and Watson, his brow furrowing as he regarded the two men with obvious disapproval. He made no attempt at a greeting, turning his attention back to Matilda. "And what about the missus? She got any fancy parties or soirees lined up?"

Matilda's discomfort was palpable, her glance flickering towards the detectives as if silently pleading for intervention. "I couldn't rightly say, Jimmy. You know how it is."

Jimmy chuckled, a low, rumbling sound that seemed to make Matilda shrink further into herself. "Aye, I reckon I do." He gestured towards the locked drawer near the stove. "Well, go on then, love. Let's have the money."

Matilda crossed to the drawer and retrieved an envelope, which she handed to Jimmy. He pocketed it without a glance, his gaze once again sweeping over her in a manner that made Holmes' jaw tighten.

"You know, Matilda," Jimmy began, "a pretty little thing like you shouldn't be cooped up in this place all day. Why don't you come out with me tonight? We'll have a bit of fun, just you and me."

Matilda's hands twisted in the fabric of her apron, her eyes downcast. "That's kind of you, Jimmy, but I really must decline. I have too much work to do here."

Jimmy's smile faded, replaced by a look of petulant annoyance. "Work, work, work. Is that all you ever think about?" He closed the distance between them with a few long strides. "You need to learn to live a little, love."

Matilda retreated until her back was against the wall, her eyes wide with apprehension. "I...I can't, Jimmy. Please, I need to get back to my duties."

Holmes rose and stepped forward, his sharp gaze fixed on Jimmy. "I believe the lady has made her position quite clear," he said, his voice calm but firm. "It would be best if you respected her wishes and took your leave."

Jimmy's eyes narrowed as he regarded Holmes, a flicker of annoyance crossing his features. For a moment, it seemed as though he might argue, but something in the detective's unwavering stare made him think better of it. With a final, dismissive snort, he turned and strode out of the kitchen; the door slamming shut behind him.

In the silence that followed, Matilda seemed to sag against the wall, her relief evident.

Holmes turned to her, his expression softening. "Are you all right?"

Matilda nodded, her hands still trembling slightly as she smoothed her apron. "Yes, thank you, Mr Holmes. I'm sorry you had to witness that."

Watson said, "Does this happen often? That man's behaviour was entirely inappropriate."

Matilda explained, "Jimmy started delivering milk here about a month ago. The previous milkman used to collect his money once a week, but Jimmy insists on collecting it daily."

Holmes' eyes narrowed thoughtfully. "And has he always been so familiar with you?"

Matilda's cheeks flushed, and she nodded. "I'm afraid so. He's over-friendly with everyone, always wanting to know everyone's business. There's something about him that makes me uneasy. Some of the other maids have mentioned it to me, too. They say he's always asking questions, trying to find out more about the families we work for."

Watson's expression darkened. "That's most concerning. A man in his position should not be prying into the affairs of others."

Holmes nodded in agreement with Dr Watson. "Matilda, could you tell me when Jimmy typically does his rounds?"

Matilda replied, "He's usually delivers the milk around five a.m., Mr Holmes. Thankfully, he leaves the bottles outside on the doorstep, so I don't have to face him at that hour. He delivers to everyone on the street, not just the Thompsons. He collects his money anywhere between three and four in the afternoon."

Holmes exchanged a meaningful glance with Watson before turning back to Matilda. "Thank you, Matilda.

You've been most helpful. If Jimmy gives you any more trouble, please don't hesitate to let us know."

Matilda smiled gratefully. "I will, Mr Holmes. Thank you."

With a nod, Holmes and Watson took their leave, stepping out into the bright sunlight of the afternoon. As they walked Holmes' brow was furrowed in thought, his mind already piecing together the fragments of information they had gathered.

"What do you make of it, Holmes?" Watson asked, keeping pace with his friend's long strides.

Holmes hummed thoughtfully. "There's something not quite right about this Jimmy character, Watson. His behaviour towards Matilda was most inappropriate, and the fact that he's been asking questions about the families on the street is certainly cause for concern."

Watson nodded in agreement. "Do you think he could be involved in the thefts?"

Holmes replied, "We can't rule it out. A man in his position would have easy access to the homes on the street, and his insistence on collecting payment daily could be a cover for something more sinister. If he is the thief, he could have easily taken a spare set of keys, had he spotted any."

"What shall we do now?" Watson asked.

"Let's call upon the other ladies who have experienced the loss of items. We shall soon see if there is a pattern to this mystery."

Chapter 5

Holmes and Watson made their way to the home of Mrs Henderson, the woman who had lost her pearl necklace.

Mrs Henderson was of similar age to Mrs Thompson and had an air of quiet elegance. She welcomed them into her sitting room and offered refreshments, which Holmes and Watson politely declined.

"Mr Holmes, Dr Watson," Mrs Henderson said as she settled into an armchair, "what brings you here today?"

Holmes explained, "We're investigating a series of suspected thefts that have occurred in the area. Mrs Thompson has reported a missing brooch, and we have reason to believe that others on this street may have experienced similar losses."

Mrs Henderson's hand flew to her throat, her eyes widening. "Goodness! Mr Holmes, only recently, I noticed my pearl necklace had gone missing. I thought I had simply misplaced it, but now that you mention suspected thefts..." She trailed off, a look of concern crossing her features.

Watson leaned forward, his voice gentle. "When did you last see the necklace, Mrs Henderson?"

"A week ago. I wore it to a dinner party and remember putting it back in my jewellery box that evening. But when I went to wear it again a few days ago, it was gone."

Holmes asked, "And have you noticed any signs of a break-in? Any disturbances or out-of-place items in your home?"

Mrs Henderson shook her head. "No, nothing at all. Everything has been quite normal, apart from the missing necklace."

Watson recorded the details in his notebook. "And when is your house typically empty?"

"Well, I often go out to visit friends or run errands in the late morning and early afternoon. My husband is at work during the day. My children have all grown and left the family home."

Holmes nodded thoughtfully. "Thank you, Mrs Henderson. This information is most helpful. Your maid, the one who showed us in, may we talk to her, please?"

"Why, of course," Mrs Henderson replied. "She'll be polishing the silver in the dining room. It's just along the hallway at the end. You can't miss it."

"Thank you." Holmes rose. "Is her name Betsy?"

Mrs Henderson's eyebrows rose. "She is. My word, Mr Holmes, how did you know that?"

Holmes smiled. "Mrs Thompson's maid told us. Does Betsy leave the house during the day at all?"

"Yes, but she always waits until I've left, in case I need anything. She's most attentive to my needs. Is there anything else you wish to know, Mr Holmes?"

"Not at the moment, thank you." He smiled. "We will try our best to return your precious pearls to you."

Mrs Henderson let out a sigh of relief. "Thank you, thank you so much."

Holmes and Watson entered the dining room a few moments later, and found Betsy diligently polishing the silver. Her movements were precise and methodical, but there was a tension in her shoulders that betrayed her unease.

Holmes approached her, his voice gentle but firm. "Betsy, we'd like to ask you a few questions, if that's okay?"

Betsy's hands stilled, and she looked up at the two men. "Of course, Mr Holmes. Is it about Mrs Henderson's missing necklace?"

Holmes nodded. "It is. What do you know about its disappearance?"

Betsy gave him a grim look. "I think it's been stolen. I don't know where or how someone got in, but I know Mrs Henderson hasn't misplaced it. She's got an amazing memory and she would never forget something like that. It makes me angry to see her so upset about that lovely necklace of hers, it really does." She resumed her polishing work, her anger transferred to the silver goblet in her hands.

Dr Watson smiled gently at the young woman and said, "We are making enquiries into its disappearance. We understand there's a new milkman, Jimmy, who's been making his rounds in the neighbourhood. Have you had any interactions with him?"

Betsy replied, "Yes, sir. He's been delivering milk here for the past month."

Holmes' eyes narrowed slightly. "And how would you describe your interactions with him?"

The maid's polishing actions grew more agitated. "He's a bit odd, if I'm being honest. Always asking questions. About me, about Mrs Henderson and her husband. It's not right, the way he pries."

Watson frowned, his concern clear. "What sort of questions does he ask?"

"He wants to know about Mrs Henderson's schedule, when she's home and when she's out. He asks about Mr Henderson's work. I've tried to keep my answers short, but he's a persistent one."

Holmes said, "And have you noticed anything unusual about his behaviour? Any patterns or inconsistencies?"

Betsy thought for a moment, her brow furrowed. "Well, there was one thing. Last week, he came by to collect his money much earlier than usual. He normally gets here late in the afternoon, but he turned up at midday. I was late setting off for the market that day. A few minutes later, and I would have left the house and missed him. When I asked him why he was early, he just laughed it off, said he had a busy day ahead."

Holmes said, "Thank you, Betsy. This information is most helpful. If you remember anything else, please don't hesitate to let us know."

Betsy nodded. "I will, Mr Holmes."

Holmes and Watson left the home of Mrs Henderson and walked along Baker Street.

Watson said, "It seems our milkman is becoming more suspicious by the moment."

Holmes replied, "Indeed, Watson. His questions are far too pointed to be mere curiosity. And the change in his money collection schedule is noteworthy. We shall have to keep a close eye on him."

They called upon the remaining friend of Mrs Thompson's, Mrs Baxter. She confirmed a pair of diamond earrings had gone missing from her home over a week ago, and despite a thorough search, she hadn't found them. Like her friends, she advised there had been no signs of forced entry to the property.

Holmes and Watson also spoke to the maid in the house, Enid, who had the same opinion about Jimmy as the others had. Enid told them Mrs Baxter usually left the house between eleven a.m. and returned later in the afternoon, And, yes, she used that time to complete errands for Mrs Baxter which involved leaving the house.

After saying goodbye to Enid, Holmes and Watson made their way along Baker Street, calling upon several other neighbours to see if anyone else was missing valuable items.

To their surprise, no one had. At least, not to their knowledge, they told Holmes and Watson.

As they walked back towards 221B Baker Street, Holmes said, "The only residents who have confirmed the loss of an item are Mrs Thompson, Mrs Henderson, and Mrs Baxter. Three friends who leave the house usually at the same time every day. Their maids are absent from the house as well, albeit for a shorter time frame. I wonder if that is why they have become targets. The thief knew they were going to be out at a certain time, and it would be safe to enter their properties during those hours. Perhaps the thief left the other properties on this street alone because there was no guarantee as to when those homes would be empty."

Watson nodded. "So, it seems the suspicion is falling upon the milkman. I must say, Holmes, I disliked that man most intensely. His manner, the way he looked at Matilda, and how he talked to her. Also, did you notice how he dismissed us with one glance?"

"I did notice. There was a flicker of resentment in his eyes, too, as if the mere sight of us was repulsive to him. Watson, let's have a coffee at that new café on the corner and discuss this further."

A short while later, Holmes and Watson sat at a small table in a quaint café on Baker Street, their minds still preoccupied with the peculiar case. The aroma of freshly brewed coffee and the gentle clatter of cups and saucers filled the air as they discussed their findings.

"It seems our milkman, Jimmy, is the most likely suspect," Holmes mused, stirring his coffee thoughtfully. "The thefts began shortly after he started his rounds in the area, and they occur during the hours when he has finished his deliveries for the day."

Watson nodded. "But how does he gain entry into the houses unnoticed? Surely, someone would have seen or heard something if he were breaking in."

Holmes replied, "I suspect Jimmy uses his morning rounds to scope out the houses, looking for weak points of entry. Perhaps he notices a loose window or a faulty lock during his deliveries."

"That's a possibility," Watson agreed. "But even so, it would be risky for him to attempt a break-in during daylight hours."

"I agree," Holmes said, his eyes glinting with a sudden realisation. "But what if he doesn't need to break in at all? Consider this, Watson: when Jimmy collects his payment from the households, perhaps on occasions he is likely left alone in the kitchen for a few minutes. That would give him ample opportunity to steal a spare key or make an imprint of one for later use."

Watson's eyes widened. "Of course! And if he's skilled at picking locks, he could easily gain entry without leaving any signs of a forced break-in. So, what's our next move, Holmes?"

Holmes smiled. "I believe it's time for me to go undercover, Watson. I shall join Jimmy on his early morning rounds and observe his behaviour. Perhaps I can catch him scouting out his next target or gain some insight into his methods."

Watson sat back, a look of concern crossing his face. "Are you sure that's wise, Holmes? If Jimmy is our thief, he may become suspicious if he notices you following him."

"Fear not, my dear Watson," Holmes said, his voice brimming with confidence. "I shall be the very picture of discretion. Jimmy will never suspect that he has the great Sherlock Holmes on his tail."

With that, the two men finished their coffee and set about making preparations for Holmes' undercover mission.

Chapter 6

Holmes rose at four a.m. the next day and set about preparing for his undercover mission. He carefully donned the attire of a railway maintenance worker, ensuring that every detail was in place. He rubbed dirt and grime onto his clothes and skin, giving himself the appearance of someone who had just finished a long night's work at the station.

With his disguise complete, Holmes slipped out of 221B Baker Street and made his way to a shadowy spot at the far end of the road. From this vantage point, he had a clear view of the street, allowing him to observe the comings and goings of the early morning deliveries.

Before long, the clopping of hooves echoed through the quiet streets. Jimmy appeared on his horse-drawn cart, laden with the day's supply of milk. Holmes watched intently as Jimmy began his rounds, delivering milk to the doorsteps of the houses along Baker Street.

As Jimmy went about his work, Holmes noticed that the milkman seemed to take an unusual interest in the buildings he passed. His attention lingered on the windows and doors, as if he were studying the layout and security of each residence.

Seizing the opportunity, Holmes emerged from the shadows and approached Jimmy with a friendly greeting, careful to change the sound of his voice. "Morning, mate. You're up and early, aren't you? I thought I was the only one out at this time."

Jimmy looked up, surprised by the sudden appearance of the dirt-covered man. "Aye, that I am. Gotta get the milk delivered before the toffs wake up, don't I?" A nasty look came over his face. "These posh folk, they don't know the meaning of a hard day's work, do they? Not like us."

Holmes nodded, playing along with the conversation. "Aye, they've got more money than sense, some of 'em."

Jimmy laughed heartily. "Too right, mate! I'll tell you something. I charge these toffs a lot more than I do in the poorer streets, and they don't even bat an eye. They've got that much money, I reckon it's only right that some of it comes my way."

"I don't blame you," Holmes said with an admiring smile at Jimmy.

"Oh, yeah," Jimmy boasted, puffing out his chest. "It's easy money, mate. These rich folk, they don't even notice a few extra pennies here and there. And if they do, they're too proper to kick up a fuss about it."

Holmes tipped his cap to Jimmy. "Good luck yo you, I say. Well, I best be on my way. I'm off home for a kip, and then I'll be back at work. Take care, mate."

Jimmy waved goodbye, a self-satisfied grin on his face. "Aye, you too."

With that, Holmes turned and headed away from Baker Street. Jimmy's boastful attitude and keen interest in the houses he serviced only strengthened Holmes' suspicions about his involvement in the recent thefts.

Chapter 7

After taking a circular route back to Baker Street, and making sure Jimmy was far away, Holmes quietly entered his lodgings, taking care not to wake his slumbering friend, Dr John Watson. He quickly changed out of his railway worker's disguise and into his usual attire, washing away the grime and dirt from his face and hands.

By the time Watson emerged from his room, Holmes was already seated in his armchair, his fingers steepled beneath his chin in contemplation. Watson, still groggy from sleep, poured himself a cup of tea and settled into the chair opposite his friend.

"I trust your early morning excursion was fruitful, Holmes?" Watson inquired, taking a sip of the hot liquid.

Holmes nodded. "It was. My conversation with Jimmy was most enlightening. It's clear he harbours a deep resentment towards the wealthy residents of Baker Street."

Watson raised an eyebrow. "Resentment? In what way?"

"He spoke of how easy it is to make a profit from the 'rich folk,' as he called them," Holmes explained. "He boasted about charging more for his services in this area than he would in poorer neighbourhoods."

"I see," Watson mused, setting his cup down. "And you believe this resentment could be a motive for the thefts?"

"It's certainly a possibility," Holmes agreed. "I've been giving this matter some thought. And I propose we lay a trap for our milkman. We must catch him in the act if we are to prove his guilt."

"And how do you suggest we go about that?" Watson asked, intrigued by his friend's plan.

"We will need Mrs Thompson's assistance. However, I believe it would be prudent to meet with her away from Baker Street. If Jimmy is our thief, he may be watching our every move."

Watson agreed, "A wise precaution, Holmes. Where do you propose we meet Mrs Thompson?"

"The art gallery a few miles from here should suffice," Holmes answered. "It's far enough away to avoid arousing suspicion, yet still easily accessible."

"When shall we contact her about this proposed meeting?" Watson asked.

"I won't contact Mrs Thompson during daylight hours in case Jimmy is nearby. I will wait until midnight, and using the cover of darkness, I will deliver a written message to Mrs Thompson, requesting her presence at the gallery tomorrow at eleven-thirty a.m."

Watson chuckled, shaking his head in admiration. "You do have a flair for the dramatic, Holmes."

"Merely a necessary precaution, my dear Watson," Holmes replied with a smile. "We must take every measure to ensure the success of our plan."

As the day progressed, Holmes and Watson went about their usual routines, careful not to draw any undue attention to themselves. They discussed the details of their plan, refining and adjusting as needed, until they were both satisfied with the course of action.

When the clock on the mantelpiece finally chimed out the midnight hour, Holmes slipped out of 221B Baker Street, a folded piece of paper tucked discreetly in his pocket. Staying in the shadows, he made his way to Mrs Thompson's residence.

With a quick glance to ensure he was unobserved, Holmes approached the front door and deftly slipped the message through the letterbox.

His task complete, Holmes melted back into the shadows, making his way home.

Chapter 8

Holmes rose early the next morning, hoping Mrs Thompson had found his note, and better still, had replied to it.

He quickly dressed and headed downstairs to check for any messages. As he approached the doorway, he noticed a small slip of paper tucked neatly into the letterbox. He quickly retrieved it.

"Ah, excellent," he murmured to himself as he read the words. "She's agreed to meet us at the gallery."

Dr Watson, still groggy from sleep, walked down the stairs, his hair tousled and his dressing gown hastily tied. "What's that, Holmes?" he asked, stifling a yawn.

"A message from Mrs Thompson," Holmes replied, holding up the note. "She's confirmed our meeting later this morning. I suggest we get there a little earlier in case our thief is hanging about outside our home. They would soon know something was up if we came out of our building at the same time as Mrs Thompson came out of hers, especially if set off in the same direction"

"Splendid idea," Watson said, his eyes brightening. "I suppose I should get dressed."

After a hearty breakfast, the two men hailed a cab and headed to the art gallery. The journey wasn't too long, and soon they found themselves standing before the impressive edifice, its stone exterior gleaming in the morning light.

They wandered around the gallery for a while, marvelling at the impressive work on display.

Mrs Thompson arrived just before eleven-thirty at the agreed meeting point within the gallery. She greeted the two men with a warm smile, though a hint of worry lingered in her eyes.

"Mr Holmes, Dr Watson," she said, extending her gloved hand. "It's good to see you again so soon."

Holmes took her hand and bowed slightly. "I trust you are well?"

"As well as can be expected, given the circumstances," she replied, her smile faltering slightly.

Watson gestured towards a nearby bench. "Shall we sit? We have much to discuss."

The three of them settled onto the bench, the hustle and bustle of the gallery's visitors fading into the background.

Holmes began, "Mrs Thompson, we believe that Jimmy, your milkman, may be responsible for the recent thefts in Baker Street."

Mrs Thompson's eyes widened as Holmes revealed his suspicions about Jimmy. She said, "I've only met the man once. Even though our meeting was brief, I didn't take to him at all. There was something about the way he looked at me. Not hateful, I think, but certainly with disdain. And you think Jimmy is the culprit?"

Holmes said, "We do. Mrs Thompson, when was the last time you wore your missing brooch?"

She furrowed her brow, her mind racing back to the events of the past few days. "It was two days before it went missing."

"And did Jimmy have the chance to see you wearing the brooch?" Holmes asked.

"Why yes! I was wearing it when I went into the kitchen to have a word with Matilda about something. It was after I'd returned home from meeting my friends, and Jimmy was there. He had come to collect the milk money. He was chatting with Matilda, although now that I think about it, he was doing all the chatting and Matilda was doing all the listening. I didn't want to discuss private business in front of him, so I told Matilda I would speak to her later and I left the kitchen."

Dr Watson said, "It's quite possible that he noticed your brooch then, Mrs Thompson. A valuable piece would certainly catch the eye of a thief."

Holmes said, "Mrs Thompson, if Jimmy is our thief, I believe we could lay a trap for him. But we will need your help."

"My help?" she asked. "What can I do?"

"We need you to wear another precious item, something that will catch Jimmy's attention when he's in the kitchen collecting his money in the afternoon," Holmes explained. "Make sure he sees it, and then leave it in your room, somewhere easy to find. Depart the house as normal the following day and stay out until your usual hour."

Mrs Thompson's face paled at the thought. "You want me to use myself as bait?"

Dr Watson said, "We understand your apprehension, Mrs Thompson, but it may be the only way to catch this thief red-handed. However, we don't want to place you in any danger. And if you don't feel comfortable doing this, please say so."

Mrs Thompson took a deep breath, her hands clasped tightly in her lap. "I suppose I can do it. I have a necklace that belonged to my mother. It's quite valuable, and yes, you're right, it would catch Jimmy's eye."

Holmes reached into his pocket and pulled out an envelope. He said, "We don't want you to use your items if case they get damaged. Inside this envelope is a fake diamond necklace. It came into our possession during a case we dealt with last year. Its value is worthless, but to the untrained eye and from a distance, it looks like the real thing. Please don't open the envelope until you get home." He lowered his voice a little. "Don't look now, but we are being observed by a security guard who is giving us suspicious looks. If you pull out the necklace now, it may look like we are passing you stolen goods."

Watson let out an almost inaudible chuckle.

Mrs Thompson took the envelope. "Thank you. I feel better about not using my own jewellery. I will go ahead with your plan this afternoon. I can't believe that man has the nerve to steal from me, and my neighbours. The sooner you catch him, the better."

Holmes nodded in agreement. "We appreciate your help, Mrs Thompson. Like I said, if you wear the item today when Jimmy collects his money, then, if he is the thief, it's likely he will enter your home tomorrow sometime between eleven a.m. and one p.m. when your house is empty. Watson and I will take up hiding positions on Baker Street and keep watch. Should Jimmy attempt to enter your home, we will be there to apprehend him."

Mrs Thompson smiled at Holmes and Watson. "I want to see this thief brought to justice. Should I tell Matilda about this plan? She'll be surprised to see me wearing an unfamiliar necklace."

Holmes pondered the matter for a moment. He said, "I think it's best we keep Matilda out of the picture for now. She might become nervous in front of Jimmy when you appear wearing the item, and then he would know something is amiss. Mrs Thompson, could you say the necklace was an impromptu gift from your husband? And that you wanted to see how it looked before placing it in your jewellery box?"

Mrs Thompson replied, "That's an excellent idea. I'll proceed on that basis. And to ensure Matilda is out for hours tomorrow, I'll give her some extra deliveries to make."

Holmes said, "Thank you, Mrs Thompson. With your help, we shall put an end to these thefts and ensure that Baker Street is safe once more."

Chapter 9

The following day, Holmes and Watson left their lodgings at ten a.m. and set out to take up their respective positions. The two men walked briskly, their faces set with determination as they prepared to catch the thief who had been plaguing the residents of the street.

"You remember the plan, Watson?" Holmes asked, his keen eyes scanning the street for any signs of suspicious activity.

"Of course, Holmes," Watson replied, patting the stack of newspapers tucked under his arm. "I'll be at the café, pretending to read while keeping a watchful eye on Mrs Thompson's house. If Jimmy shows up, I'll be ready."

Holmes nodded. "Excellent. But do keep in mind that Jimmy may be in disguise. He's a devious one, that milkman."

Watson chuckled, adjusting his hat. "I've no doubt about that, Holmes. But I suspect, even in disguise, Jimmy is the kind of man who would have an arrogant swagger. A man like that can't help but show his true colours."

"Indeed," Holmes agreed, his eyes twinkling with amusement. "Well, I shall be at the rear of Mrs Thompson's house, keeping watch from there. If Jimmy attempts to gain entry there, I'll be ready to apprehend him."

With a final nod, the two men parted ways, each focused on their assigned tasks. Watson crossed the street and entered the café, settling himself at a table near the window with his newspapers spread out before him. He ordered a cup of tea and a scone, doing his best to appear as a regular patron engrossed in the day's news.

Meanwhile, Holmes made his way to the back of Mrs Thompson's house, his sharp gaze taking in every detail of the surrounding area. As he approached it, he spotted a familiar figure tending to some flower pots in the backyard of his house, which was directly opposite Mrs Thompson's.

"Ernest!" Holmes called out, waving to his neighbour and friend. "Good morning, my dear fellow. I was hoping to catch you in."

Ernest, a kindly older gentleman with a twinkle in his eye, looked up and smiled broadly. "Sherlock Holmes!

What a pleasant surprise. I don't usually see you around the back of Baker Street. What brings you here?"

Holmes stepped closer, lowering his voice. "I'm afraid I'm here on a rather serious matter. I'm conducting a surveillance operation, attempting to catch a thief who has been targeting the homes on Baker Street. And I need your help with this case."

Ernest's eyes widened. "A thief? Well, that simply won't do. How can I be of assistance?"

Holmes smiled. "I was hoping I might use your backyard as a vantage point. I need a clear view of the rear of Mrs Thompson's house. I can conceal myself in the shadow cast by the sun across your yard; a shadow that will elongate as the day passes on."

"Of course, of course!" Ernest exclaimed, already opening the garden gate to allow Holmes to enter. "But why stop at the backyard? Come inside, my boy. You can use the bedroom window upstairs. It has a much better view of the backstreet, and the net curtain will keep you well hidden."

Holmes' eyebrows rose, impressed by Ernest's suggestion. "That's a splendid idea. Thank you."

As they entered the house, Ernest suddenly snapped his fingers. "Oh, and I have just the thing to help you with your surveillance!" He hurried over to a nearby shelf and retrieved a pair of binoculars. "I use these for my bird watching, you see. But I have a feeling they'll serve you well today."

Holmes accepted the binoculars with a grateful smile. "Perfect! Thank you."

The two men went upstairs, and Ernest showed Holmes to the bedroom window. Holmes positioned himself carefully, adjusting the binoculars to get a clear view of the back street and Mrs Thompson's house.

"I'll be downstairs if you need anything," Ernest said, giving his friend a supportive pat on the shoulder. "Best of luck catching that scoundrel."

"Thank you, Ernest," Holmes replied. "With any luck, we'll have our thief in custody before the day is through."

As Ernest left the room, Holmes settled in for what he hoped would be a productive surveillance operation. With Watson watching the front of the house and himself keeping an eye on the rear, they had all the bases covered. Now, it was simply a matter of waiting for Jimmy to make his move.

Chapter 10

Holmes focused his keen gaze on the backstreet behind Baker Street, watching the comings and goings of various people.

He noticed a young woman carrying a basket of laundry, a boy delivering newspapers, and an elderly gentleman walking his dog. He had no idea people used the backstreet so much.

A soft knock at the door drew Holmes' attention away from the window. Ernest entered the room, carrying a tray with a steaming cup of tea and a slice of cake.

"Thought you might need a little something to keep your energy up," he said with a smile.

"That's very kind of you," Holmes replied, accepting the tea and cake with a grateful nod.

Ernest set the tray down on a nearby table and glanced out the window. "Any sign of the scoundrel yet?"

Holmes shook his head. "Not yet. But I have a feeling he'll show his face soon enough."

"Is there anything I can do to help?" Ernest asked, his eyes twinkling with excitement at the prospect of being involved in one of Sherlock Holmes' cases.

Holmes took a sip of his tea and said, "Actually, I'm keeping an eye out for the milkman. He's a suspect in our current case."

Ernest's face darkened. "Oh, I know exactly who you mean. That Jimmy fellow, right? Can't stand the man, myself. Always talking down to me like I'm some sort of fool. Several of the neighbours have complained about him too. In fact, I've already lodged a complaint with the dairy he works for. Wouldn't be surprised if he's been sacked already."

Holmes frowned, a hint of concern crossing his features. "If he's been sacked, he may not show up today. Which means he has got away with his previous thefts."

Ernest shook his head. "Don't you worry about that. Bad pennies always turn up somewhere. If he's guilty, you'll catch him."

Holmes smiled, reassured by his friend's confidence. He turned his attention back to the street below, just in time to see Matilda, Mrs Thompson's maid, leaving the house through the back door. He watched as she carefully locked the door behind her. She pulled the hood of her cloak over her head and set off down the street, her stride purposeful.

The minutes ticked by as Holmes maintained his vigil, his attention never leaving the backstreet. He watched as the shadows lengthened and the activity in the street began to dwindle. But still, there was no sign of Jimmy.

Ernest, who had been sitting quietly in a chair near the window, broke the silence. "Sherlock, do you think he might have caught wind of your investigation? Maybe he's decided to lay low for a while."

Holmes considered this for a moment. "It's possible. But I have a feeling he's too arrogant to believe he could be caught. No, I think he'll show his face, eventually. We just need to be patient."

Chapter 11

One hour later, and with his attention still focused intently on the backstreet, Holmes was surprised to see Matilda returning to Mrs Thompson's house much earlier than expected. He checked his pocket watch. It was midday. She shouldn't be back until at least one o'clock. Mrs Thompson said she'd give Matilda extra duties to make sure the house was empty for long enough for a theft to occur. Why had she come back so early? And was she about to sabotage the carefully laid plan he had put in place?

As he watched Matilda approach the house, Holmes' suspicions began to grow. Could it be that Matilda, and not Jimmy, was behind the recent string of thefts?

It was true that Matilda had easy access to the valuable items within. Perhaps, Holmes mused, she had returned early to steal the diamond necklace he'd given to Mrs Thompson. Once the necklace was in her possession,

Matilda could easily take it to the nearest pawnbroker and then return to the house at her usual time of one o'clock in the afternoon, as if nothing had happened.

But what about the thefts from Mrs Henderson and Mrs Baxter's homes? Holmes' mind raced as he considered the possibilities. Could Matilda have somehow obtained spare keys to those residences as well? Perhaps she had visited those friends of hers who worked there as maids and managed to pilfer a spare set of keys during her visits.

As Holmes pondered these thoughts, his gaze never wavered from the Mrs Thompson's house. He watched as Matilda emerged five minutes later, her movements quick and furtive. He looked closer. There was something different about the way she was walking and the tilt of her head. Suddenly, a realisation struck him like a bolt of lightning. The person he had assumed to be Matilda was not the maid at all, but it was someone disguised as her.

Holmes' heart raced as he processed this new information.

He turned to Ernest and said, "I have spotted the culprit! I must go!"

With that, Holmes hurried out of the room, raced down the steps and out of Ernest's house, his heart pounding with the thrill of the chase. His keen eyes locked onto the figure disguised as Matilda, who was now hurrying down the street with a sense of urgency that betrayed their guilt.

"Stop right there!" Holmes called out, his voice ringing through the narrow alleyway.

The imposter glanced over their shoulder, their eyes widening in surprise and fear as they saw the detective in hot pursuit. Without a moment's hesitation, they broke into a run, their skirts billowing behind them as they fled.

Holmes gave chase, his long strides quickly closing the distance between them.

The imposter darted around the corner, disappearing from view for a moment. Holmes followed.

The chase led them past the café where Dr John Watson sat, gazing out of the window, a newspaper in his hands. The sound of running footsteps and Holmes' shouts caught his attention. He saw his friend, and the disguised figure sprinting by.

Without hesitation, Watson threw down his newspaper and leapt to his feet, abandoning his half-finished cup of tea on the table. He dashed out of the café and joined the pursuit.

The imposter, realising they now had two pursuers, redoubled their efforts to escape. They wove through the crowded streets, pushing past startled pedestrians and narrowly avoiding collisions with horse-drawn carriages.

Holmes and Watson, undeterred by the obstacles in their path, maintained their relentless pursuit.

As they raced down a particularly narrow alleyway, the imposter made a desperate attempt to evade capture. They overturned a stack of wooden crates, sending them tumbling into the path of their pursuers.

Holmes, with his lightning-fast reflexes, leapt over the fallen crates, barely breaking his stride. Watson, however, was not so fortunate. He stumbled, his foot catching on a splintered piece of wood, and he fell to the ground with a grunt of pain.

Holmes, torn between his desire to apprehend the suspect and his concern for his friend, hesitated for a split second. But Watson, ever the loyal companion, waved him on, urging him to continue the chase.

With a nod of understanding, Holmes pressed on, his determination renewed. He could hear the imposter's laboured breathing ahead of him, a sign that they were tiring from the relentless pursuit.

As they emerged from the alleyway onto a bustling main street, Holmes saw his chance. With a final burst of speed, he lunged forward, his hand outstretched. His fingers closed around the imposter's arm, and he yanked them to a halt, spinning them around to face him.

The imposter, their disguise now dishevelled and their face flushed with exertion, glared at Holmes with a mixture of defiance and fear. But the detective's gaze was unwavering, his expression one of grim satisfaction.

"The game is up," Holmes declared, his voice steady despite his own breathlessness. "It's time to reveal your true identity and face the consequences of your actions."

As the imposter's shoulders slumped in defeat, Watson, having recovered from his fall, joined Holmes' side.

Holmes reached for the hood that covered the imposter's face.

Chapter 12

Holmes pulled back the hood, revealing the face of Betsy, Mrs Henderson's maid.

"By Jove!" Watson exclaimed. "I was expecting to see you."

"Betsy," Holmes said, his voice gentle but firm, "are you the one who has been committing these thefts?"

Betsy's eyes welled up with tears, and she nodded, her voice barely above a whisper. "Yes, Mr Holmes. It was me. I never meant for it to go this far, but I was desperate."

Holmes said, "Tell us what happened. What drove you to such desperate measures?"

With a shaky breath, Betsy began her story. "It's my mother, sir. She's been ill for some time now, and the medical bills are piling up. I've been working as hard as I can to pay them, but it's never enough. The cost of her treatment is so high, and I didn't know what else to do."

Holmes nodded, his expression one of understanding. "And so, you turned to theft."

"I never wanted to be a thief," Betsy cried, her tears now flowing freely. "It started when I was visiting Enid, the maid at Mrs Baxter's house. I went upstairs to use the bathroom, and as I passed Mrs Baxter's bedroom, I saw some diamond earrings just sitting there. It was like they were calling to me, promising a solution to all my problems."

Watson said, "So you took them and pawned them to pay for your mother's treatment?"

"Yes," Betsy admitted, her voice filled with shame. "And it worked. I was able to pay for her medicine, but then she took a turn for the worse. I knew I needed more money, and that's when I stole from Mrs Henderson, my own employer. I'm so very ashamed, after all she's done for me. But I couldn't stop myself."

Holmes said, "And you stole from Mrs Thompson, too. How did you manage that?"

Betsy answered, "I had to deliver a message to Matilda earlier this week, and when she left the kitchen, I noticed some spare keys hanging up, so I took a set. I didn't want to, but all I could think about was Mum. She's the only family I've got and I can't lose her. I used those keys to get into the house when I knew Matilda would be out, and I took Mrs Thompson's brooch. I took her diamond necklace, too, just now. Matilda told me about it when we met at the shops earlier. I knew it would be enough to cover the rest of my mother's treatment. I told myself it would be the last time that I'd never steal again."

Watson said, "Oh, Betsy. I can't imagine the desperation you must have felt, but surely there were other options? Why didn't you ask for help?"

"I was too ashamed," Betsy said, her voice breaking. "I didn't want anyone to know about my mother's illness or our financial troubles. I thought I could handle it on my own, but it just got worse and worse."

Holmes said gently, "Betsy, I understand the desperation that drove you to these actions, but you must know that theft is never the answer. There are always consequences, and now you must face them."

Betsy nodded, her face streaked with tears. "I know. I'm ready to accept whatever punishment I deserve. I just hope that somehow, my mother will be taken care of."

Chapter 13

Later that afternoon, Sherlock Holmes and Dr John Watson returned to their lodgings at 221B Baker Street, their minds still preoccupied with the events of the day. As they settled into their respective armchairs, Mrs Hudson, bustled into the room, a look of concern upon her face.

"Mr Holmes, Dr Watson," she began, "have you solved the case yet? Or should I still be fretting about a thief lurking on our very doorstep?"

Holmes said, "I am pleased to say that the culprit has been apprehended, and the stolen items have been recovered."

Mrs Hudson exclaimed, "Oh, thank heavens! But who was behind it all?"

Watson answered, "It was Betsy, the maid who works for Mrs Henderson."

Mrs Hudson let out a gasp. "Betsy? That lovely young woman? No! Why would she do such a thing?"

Holmes explained, "Betsy's mother is gravely ill, and the cost of her medical treatment had become an overwhelming burden. In a moment of desperation, Betsy succumbed to the temptation of theft, believing it to be her only means of providing for her mother's care. She soon committed further thefts in order to raise more funds."

Mrs Hudson shook her head. "Oh, the poor dear. I can't imagine the desperation she must have felt to resort to such measures."

Watson said, "Indeed, Mrs Hudson. It's a tragic situation all around."

"But what will happen to Betsy now?" Mrs Hudson asked.

Holmes said, "That, I'm afraid, is for the victims of her crime to decide. They may take pity on her plight, but they might not, considering the value of the items stolen and the heartache it has caused them."

Mrs Hudson nodded, her expression thoughtful. "I suppose you're right, Mr Holmes. It's a difficult position for all involved."

Holmes continued, "Watson and I visited the pawnbrokers Betsy had used to sell the stolen items. Fortunately, they were still available for purchase. I informed the shop owner that the items in question were stolen property and needed to be returned to their rightful owners."

Watson chuckled. "The owner was none too pleased, but Holmes was quite insistent."

"Once we had the items in hand," Holmes continued, "we took Betsy and the recovered pieces to Mrs Henderson's residence and explained the situation. It is now up to Mrs Henderson and her friends to decide whether they wish to involve the authorities."

Mrs Hudson said, "Well, I do hope they show some mercy. Betsy's actions were wrong, of course, but her motivations were borne out of love and desperation."

Holmes said, "On a lighter note, one of the more satisfying aspects of this investigation was witnessing the dismissal of that dreadful milkman, Jimmy."

Mrs Hudson's eyes lit up. "Oh, yes! I heard about that from Vera next door. Apparently, many residents had lodged numerous complaints about his behaviour."

Watson said, "And rightly so. The man was an absolute menace."

Holmes said, "It seems that even in the midst of such a troubling case, there are small victories to be celebrated."

Mrs Hudson smiled. "Well, I'm just glad that the mystery has been solved and that our street is safe once more. Thank you, Mr Holmes, Dr Watson, for all your hard work."

Mrs Hudson left the room looking much happier than when she had entered.

Holmes said to Watson, "Of course, I am pleased we discovered who the culprit was, but the reasons behind the crime sadden me."

Watson said, "That aspect has been bothering me, too. As such, I intend to call upon Betsy's mother later today and offer my medical services free of charge."

Holmes' eyebrows rose. "You would do that? Watson, you are a gentleman in the truest sense of the word. I am proud to call you my friend. I am a fortunate fellow to have you in my life."

Watson cleared his throat. "Now don't get all emotional on me, Holmes. You know it doesn't suit you."

Sherlock Holmes burst into laughter. "You are right about that, but even I can let my emotions get the better of me sometimes." He smiled at his friend, a twinkle in his eyes. "I'll try not to let it happen again."

* Read on for a preview of the next book in this series, Sherlock Holmes and The Lamplighter's Mystery

A note from the author

For as long as I can remember, I have loved reading mystery books. It started with Enid Blyton's Famous Five, and The Secret Seven. As I got older, I progressed to Agatha Christie books, and of course, Sir Arthur Conan Doyle's Sherlock Holmes.

I love the characters of Sherlock Holmes and Dr Watson, and the Victorian era that the stories are set in. It seemed only natural that one day, I would write some of my own Sherlock stories. I love creating new mysteries for Mr Holmes, and his trusty companion, Dr John Watson. It's not just the era itself that seems to ignite ideas within me; it's also the characters who were around at that time, and the lives they led.

This story has been checked for errors, but if you see anything we have missed and you'd like to let us know about them, please email mabel@mabelswift.com

You can hear about my new releases by signing up to my newsletter As a thank you for subscribing, I will send you a free short story: Sherlock Holmes and The Curious Clock.

If you'd like to contact me, you can get in touch via mabel@mabelswift.com I'd be delighted to hear from you.

Best wishes

Mabel

Sherlock Holmes and the Lamplighter's Mystery - a preview

Chapter 1

The rain pattered against the windows of 221B Baker Street, the sound a gentle accompaniment to the crackling fire in the hearth. Sherlock Holmes sat in his armchair, long fingers steepled beneath his chin, his grey eyes fixed on some distant point. Dr John Watson, as was his habit, busied himself with the day's newspaper, occasionally tutting at some article or another.

A sharp knock at the door roused both men from their respective reveries. Mrs Hudson, Holmes's long-suffering landlady, entered, her expression one of mild apology. "A Mr Percy Wentworth to see you, Mr Holmes. He seems quite distressed."

Holmes straightened, a glint of interest in his eye. "Send him in, Mrs Hudson."

Moments later, a man entered the room. He was in his early fifties, with a lean, agile frame that spoke of a life of physical labour. His clothes, though well-worn, were clean and neatly patched. He removed his cap, twisting it nervously in his hands.

"Mr Holmes, Dr Watson," he began, "I apologise for the intrusion, but I didn't know where else to turn."

Watson gestured to a chair. "Please, sit down, Mr Wentworth. Tell us what troubles you."

Wentworth sat, perching on the edge of the seat. "It's my job, sirs. I've been a lamplighter for nigh on thirty years, and I've never had a problem like this before."

Holmes leaned forward, his attention fully captured. "Go on."

"Someone's been sabotaging my work," Wentworth said, his hands clenching around his cap. "Lamps that I know I've lit, they're out again when I check on them later.

And my tools, they go missing, or I find them broken. I'm falling behind on my rounds, and I'm afraid I'll lose my job."

Watson frowned. "Have you reported this to your superiors?"

Wentworth shook his head miserably. "What can I tell them? That I'm suddenly incapable of doing the job I've done for decades? They'll think I've gone mad, or that I'm too old for the work."

Holmes steepled his fingers once more. "You mentioned 'someone'. Have you seen this person?"

Wentworth hesitated, then nodded. "A few times, I've spotted a figure lurking in the shadows. Always at night, always when I'm on my rounds. But when they realise I've seen them, they run off. I've never got a clear look at them."

The detective's eyes narrowed. "And this, combined with the sabotage, has led to your current state of distress?"

"I haven't slept in days," Wentworth admitted. "I'm jumping at every shadow, expecting to see that figure. And the thought of losing my job, well, it's too much."

Watson, his face etched with sympathy, turned to his friend. "Holmes, surely we can help?"

Holmes was silent for a few moments, his gaze distant. Finally, he said, "Mr Wentworth, we will take your case.

I cannot abide a mystery, and this one presents several intriguing points. The identity of your shadowy stalker, and the motive behind the sabotage. Yes, this is something we can help you with."

Relief washed over Wentworth's face. "Thank you, Mr Holmes. Thank you."

Holmes said, "Mr Wentworth, we will need more details about your work. Your nightly rounds, your duties, anything that might shed light on this mystery."

Wentworth nodded, a glimmer of pride entering his eyes as he spoke of his profession. "Of course. As a lamplighter, it's my job to ensure the gas lamps in my assigned area are lit at dusk and extinguished at dawn. I'm responsible for maintaining the lamps, too. Cleaning the glass, replacing the mantles, and making sure there's enough gas. It's not an easy job, sirs. We're out in all weathers, and the hours are long. But there's a satisfaction in it, knowing you're helping to keep the city safe and bright."

Watson, ever the empathetic listener, nodded. "I can imagine. And your rounds, Mr Wentworth? Do you follow the same route each night?"

Wentworth sat up a little straighter. "Yes, Dr Watson. I'm responsible for the lamps around the Downing Street area. Those streets are where many government offices are situated, and some people inside them work all hours, sometimes into the night. It's imperative that the lamps are in good working order. I've been doing that area for ten years now. It's one of the most important rounds in London. I know of many lamplighters who would love to be in charge of those lamps. Which makes this sabotage business even worse. I don't want to lose that round, not when I've worked so hard to make it mine."

"And your colleagues, your supervisors, what do they think of your work?" Holmes asked.

A touch of colour appeared in Wentworth's cheeks. "Well, I don't like to boast, Mr Holmes, but I'm well-respected in the company. I've always been diligent, you see. Never missed a shift, never had a complaint. I take pride in my work, and I think that shows. And I always make sure my record book is up to date. It's where I make notes about my rounds. The times when I lit and extinguished the lamps, and any repairs I had to make, that sort of thing. My record book is my most important possession and I take great care of it. My supervisors are always impressed with how efficient I am at keeping detailed notes." He fidgeted with his cap, his gaze dropping to the floor. "That's why this business has me so rattled. I can't bear the thought of them thinking I'm slipping, that I can't do my job anymore."

Watson reached out, patting Wentworth's shoulder reassuringly. "We understand, Mr Wentworth. And we'll do everything we can to get to the bottom of this."

Holmes, meanwhile, had risen and was pacing the room, his brow furrowed in thought. "The tools of your trade, Mr Wentworth, where do you store them when you're not using them?"

Wentworth blinked, surprised by the question. "In the alley behind my lodgings. There's a storage area at the end of it. It's where some of the other lamplighters keep their equipment, too. I keep my toolbox there, and my ladders as well."

Holmes nodded, a glint in his eye. "I see. And have you noticed anything unusual there? Any signs of disturbance or tampering?"

Wentworth frowned, thinking. "Now that I know of. My ladder is always where I leave it. And my toolbox too. Unless I've missed something obvious."

Holmes said, "It is possible that in your tired state, you may, indeed, have missed something. Perhaps some vital clue that the shadowy saboteur has left behind. This gives us a starting point. Mr Wentworth, I will need the address of your lodgings, and your permission to examine the storage area."

Wentworth, looking somewhat bewildered, nodded. "Of course, Mr Holmes. Anything you need. As it happens, I'm heading back home now."

"Excellent!" Holmes declared. "Then we shall come with you and start our investigation immediately. We will have your mystery cleared up in no time at all, Mr Wentworth."

Chapter 2

As the trio walked through the bustling streets of London, Percy Wentworth led the way, his shoulders hunched against the drizzling rain. Sherlock Holmes and Dr John Watson followed close behind.

After a brisk ten-minute walk, they arrived at a narrow, nondescript building tucked away in a side street.

"This is it," Wentworth said, gesturing towards a wooden door. "My lodgings."

He led them down a cramped alley that ran alongside the building. The space was barely wide enough for two people to walk abreast; the cobblestones slick with rain and grime. At the end of the alley, they came to a small, walled-off area.

"This is where we keep our equipment," Wentworth explained as he opened the door to the area.

Holmes stepped into the storage area, taking in every detail of the scene. It was cluttered with various tools and implements, such as ladders, toolboxes, coils of rope, and spare lantern parts. A low brick wall enclosed the space, but it would have been easy enough for someone to climb over, especially under the cover of darkness.

Watson, too, was examining the scene with a critical eye. "It doesn't seem very secure," he commented. "Anyone could access this area, especially if the door is left unlocked, as it was now."

Wentworth said, "There's never any need to lock it. We trust each other." He paused. "Or we used to, but I'm starting to think otherwise now, what with my damaged and lost tools."

Holmes crouched down, running his fingers over the ground. "There are several sets of footprints here. Difficult to distinguish with the rain, but it's clear this area sees regular traffic." Rising, he said, "Your ladder, Mr Wentworth. Which one is it?"

Wentworth pointed to a tall wooden ladder leaning against the wall.

Holmes approached it, running his hands over the rungs and examining the joints. "No obvious signs of damage or tampering," he said after a moment. "Now, where is your toolbox? I can see several here."

Wentworth said, "I keep mine tucked behind my ladder."

"Ah, yes, I see." Holmes examined the battered toolbox, which was locked. "Again, there are no signs of tampering. But that doesn't mean much. A clever saboteur would know how to cover their tracks. I assume your toolbox is always kept locked?"

Wentworth nodded. "It is." He gave them a wry smile. "But it's not the best of locks. I've had it for years and I think it's more rust than metal now."

Holmes shot him a smile. "Perhaps it's time for a new lock. Could we see your room? And the records you mentioned?"

Wentworth led them back out of the alley and into the building. They climbed a narrow, creaking staircase to the third floor, where he unlocked a door and ushered Holmes and Watson into a small, sparsely furnished room.

"It's not much," the lamplighter said apologetically, "but it's home."

Watson looked around, taking in the narrow bed, the washstand, the small table and chair. A single window looked out over the rooftops of London. It was a humble abode, but clean and well-kept.

Wentworth went to the table and picked up a leather-bound book. "These are my records," he said, handing it to Holmes. "Every lamp I've lit, every repair I've made, it's all in here. My route details are in it, too."

Holmes flipped through the pages, his eyes scanning the neat, precise entries. "You keep very detailed accounts, Mr Wentworth."

A hint of pride entered Percy's voice. "I have to. The Lamplighter's Office requires it. We have to submit our records every month for review."

Watson frowned. "And what happens if there are discrepancies? If a lamplighter falls behind on their duties?"

Percy's face darkened. "It's not good, Dr Watson. The Lamplighter's Office takes a very dim view of any failings. If a lamplighter isn't doing their job properly, they can be dismissed. And that's not all I have to worry about. I'm a member of The Lamplighter's Union, and they send inspectors around to check on our records, sometimes without any warning. And if the inspectors find anything amiss, they'll let the Lamplighter's Office know. Again, it could be a reason for dismissal."

Holmes handed the book back to Wentworth. "Now, if you could walk us through your nightly routine. Every detail, if you please. The more we know, the better equipped we'll be to unravel this mystery."

"Of course, Mr Holmes. It all starts when I arrive at the yard to collect my equipment. I make a note of what time I do that. Let me show you." Wentworth flipped through the pages of his record book. His eyes suddenly widened in disbelief. "This isn't right! Someone has been in my room, tampering with my records! Look, you can see how they've made it look as if I left for work later than I did, and that I returned too early. This isn't right at all! If an inspector turns up to look at this book without any warning, I'll be in real trouble, that's for sure."

Holmes walked slowly around the room. He examined the door and windows, searching for any signs of forced entry, but found none. The lock on the door was old but sturdy, and the windows were latched from the inside.

"No obvious signs of a break-in," he said, his brow furrowed in thought. "Which suggests that whoever did this either had a key or was let in. Mr Wentworth, I need you to think carefully. Is there anyone who might have a grudge against you? Another lamplighter, perhaps, someone who lives in this building or nearby?"

Wentworth hesitated for a few moments before saying, "Well, there's Horace Cuthbert. He's been a lamplighter for about ten years. He's always arguing with everyone, often for no reason at all. A real grumpy sort, and selfish too. And Horace has been after my route for years. He's made no secret of that. I get the feeling he's also jealous of how well-liked I am at the company."

Holmes nodded. "And where does Mr Cuthbert live?"

"Just down the street," Wentworth replied. "But surely it couldn't be him? I mean, Horace is a difficult man, but to go this far?"

Holmes held up a hand. "We must not rule out any possibilities, Mr Wentworth. Jealousy and resentment can drive men to desperate acts. We need to approach this carefully. If Mr Cuthbert is indeed behind this, we will need proof. Solid, irrefutable proof."

Watson added, "And we must act quickly. If those altered records are seen by someone in an official capacity by one of those inspectors you mentioned, well..." He didn't need to finish the sentence. The consequences hung heavy in the air.

Wentworth slumped down onto his bed, his face pale. "What am I going to do? I don't want to lose my job. It means the world to me."

Holmes turned to face the distressed lamplighter. "You're not going to lose your job, Mr Wentworth. I give you my word. We will solve this mystery. And soon. Do you have Mr Cuthbert's address?"

Wentworth said, "I do. He'll be starting his rounds soon. Shall I give you those details as well?"

"Please," Watson said.

Once they had the required information, Holmes said, "We will take our leave, Mr Wentworth, but we will be in touch soon." He tipped his hat in farewell and left the room with Watson at his side.

***

Sherlock Holmes and The Lamplighter's Mystery is now available on Amazon.

Printed in Great Britain
by Amazon